# Split Ends!

Adapted by Robin Wasserman

Based on "The Party" and "The Secret"
Teleplays by Sue Rose and Madellaine Paxson

Based on *Unfabulous* created by Sue Rose

**SCHOLASTIC INC.**

New York    Toronto    London    Auckland    Sydney
Mexico City    New Delhi    Hong Kong    Buenos Aires

12 11 10 9 8 7 6 5 4 3 2 1                                        5 6 7 8 9/0

Printed in the U.S.A.
First printing, November 2005

Ever wonder what your school would look like if all the students just mysteriously disappeared? Think about it — all those noisy, crowded hallways suddenly empty, abandoned. An eerie silence settling over the darkened classrooms. A few teachers wandering aimlessly through the halls, looking for students to teach. After all, what's a school without students?

Well, you can wonder all you like, but I *know* — because I've seen it.

It was a bright and sunny Friday afternoon at Rocky Road Middle School. An afternoon like any other — except for one thing. The students were gone. Vanished.

What had happened, you may ask, to put the world so out of whack that a regular middle school became a ghost town? Was there an outbreak of monkey pox? Had the student body been kidnapped by aliens?

Worse.

It was . . . PICTURE DAY.

For one day only, the yearbook photographer was set up in the front lobby, ready to immortalize us forever. Which meant, for one day only, the entire student body had fled. As far away and as fast as possible. Only two students were clueless enough, or perfect enough, to show up.

Picture day wasn't always like this. I mean, it used to be fun. I actually looked forward to it. Can you imagine? But that was before. When life was less complicated and I didn't know that I wasn't fabulous.

There was a time when I thought I was as photogenic as a model. Everyone said so. Well . . . okay, my grandmother said so. She's always telling me, "Addie, you're pretty as a princess" — even when she's looking at a picture of me in my kiddie softball uniform. I'd just slid into third base. Headfirst. Yeah. Kiddie softball was not good for me. But my grandmother told me I looked beautiful, and I believed her.

We have picture day every year, and every year, I get dressed up in my coolest outfit, spend about ten

2

seconds longer than usual on my hair, and I'm ready to go. No second thoughts, no questions asked. Every year, that is, until this year. There I was in seventh grade, and something — *everything* — was different.

So what happened? How did I get from loving the camera to panicking at the sight of it? How did I go from saying "Cheese!" to saying "No, please!"?

Well, it's not like I just woke up one day and decided I was totally unphotogenic. No, it's a much longer story than that. Lucky for you, I have some time on my hands.

It started out like a totally regular day. I was late, Geena got busted for wearing a skirt that was too short, and Zach wore a shirt that smelled like wet hay.

"Zach, could you move away from the window?" Geena asked as we sat in homeroom waiting for the day to officially start. "Whenever there's a breeze, I throw up a little in my mouth."

"What you're smelling is raw alfalfa," Zach announced proudly. He leaned over toward Geena's desk to offer her a closer look at his shirt. She pulled back so quickly she nearly fell off the other side of her chair. "If more people wore it, there wouldn't be a hole in the ozone."

Geena's look said: *Better a hole in the ozone than a world of fashion victims smelling like rotten vegetables.* But don't worry, she said it (silently) with love. The three of us have been friends for a *long* time, and we've

4

come to tolerate one another's little weirdnesses. Geena thinks she's America's next top fashion designer, Zach thinks he's Gandhi, and I . . . well, I think they're the coolest people I know. Which I guess makes me the weirdest one of all.

Anyway, like I said, it was a totally regular day. And I had no reason to believe that it wouldn't end like a totally regular day.

And then came the morning announcements.

"An important announcement regarding yearbook photos," Principal Brandywine began, her voice crackling through our ancient PA system. The whole class sat forward on the edge of our seats — picture day was, of course, a big deal. I mean, don't get me wrong, posterity is all well and good — but I'm also all for a cutie like Jake Behari spotting my picture and thinking, *Dude, Addie Singer's pretty as a princess!*

"The school board has decided to move picture day," Principal Brandywine continued. "The photographer will give us a better price if we don't compete with spring weddings or Cinco de Mayo. Therefore, picture day will now be this Friday."

I whirled around in my seat, already knowing what I would see: Geena, in full panic mode.

"What?" she squealed. "I'm not prepared!" Then

5

she gave herself a little shake and took a deep breath, trying to pull herself together. "It's okay, it's okay," she assured herself. "I'll just take my picture on the make-up day."

Good idea, except . . .

"Due to our limited budget," Principal Brandywine said, "there will be no makeup day. If you are not here on Friday, your picture will *not* appear in the yearbook."

Not appear in the yearbook? But that would be like fading from the historical record. How would you even know you'd existed? And what would go in its place — just a big, blank white space of nothingness?

"Instead, the spot where your picture should have been will be filled with a haiku of your choosing," Principal Brandywine explained, as if she could read my thoughts from all the way down in the principal's office. "If you do not choose a haiku, one will be chosen for you."

I've got a haiku for her:

*Ruining our days,*
*That Principal Brandywine.*
*What will she do next?*

It was the right number of syllables, but somehow, I figured I was better off sticking with the photo.

Just when we thought the announcements were over, there was a high-pitched whine and the speakers crackled back to life.

"Remember to *dress appropriately*!" Principal Brandywine snapped, enunciating every syllable carefully so we'd be sure to catch her meaning. "You are students of a hallowed institution, *not* half-starved urchins posing for a fashion catalog!"

Geena slumped down in her chair and put her head in her hands. "How am I supposed to pull together the one look that says 'Me in Seventh Grade' in just three days?" she asked in desperation.

Even Zach was knocked for a loop.

"If I get my hair cut now," he mused, rubbing a hand lightly across the top of his head, "I'll reek of the 'Dork Who Got His Hair Cut Especially for Picture Day' look."

"Yeah," Geena agreed, stifling a gag as she got another whiff of his alfalfa shirt. "*Reek*." I could tell she didn't think Zach really understood the magnitude of her problem — after all, no matter what he does, his hair always looks the same. Besides, it's different for guys.

Of course, it was different for me, too. I gave Geena a polite "Sorry, but I don't feel your pain" smile.

But what can I say? Picture day had just never been a problem for me. If there was one place I felt confident, it was in front of the camera.

As the homeroom bell rang and we trooped out of the classroom, I followed Geena and Zach. They were still complaining about picture day, so I zoned out and started thinking about some of my greatest photo-graphic hits. Our photo albums at home are just filled with so many fabulous pictures of me, where should I begin? There was that shot of our family vacation at the Grand Canyon — the rest of the family all looked like they hadn't showered in days, but I was glowing like I'd just stepped out of a fashion spread in *Campground Cosmo*. Then, of course, there was that windy day at the amusement park where I posed with the guy in a giant bear suit. So what if the wind had blown a piece of trash into his face? *I* looked spectacular. But I think my all-time favorite picture of myself has always been one from a few years ago, where I'm sitting on Santa's lap. Santa's got some serious red-eye — while I look like I'm ready to star in the *Nutcracker*. You have to admit, it takes a pretty photogenic kid to make *Santa* look bad.

As we got to our lockers, Zach and Geena were

still freaking out. They only stopped when Zach's friend Mario showed up.

"Geena, if you see Zach, can you tell him I'll meet him at basketball practice?" Mario asked.

Zach wrinkled his nose in confusion and exaggeratedly waved at Mario, who was standing only a foot away. Close enough to see Zach — not to mention *smell* him.

"Oh, sorry," Mario added with a smirk. "Didn't see you there. So what do you call that color," he asked, gesturing at Zach's alfalfa shirt, "dirty locker green?"

"You're funny," Zach said sulkily. I stifled a giggle. It was true, Zach's shirt was almost exactly the same vomitous color as our lockers. Standing up against them, his torso just faded into the background. He looked kind of like a head floating in midair.

"I know," Mario agreed, taking Zach's sarcasm seriously. "Anyway," he continued, still laughing at his own joke, "I just heard that the new uniforms are here."

"Sweet!" Zach exclaimed, exchanging a high five with Mario. "Now we'll look like a *real* team."

It was true that wearing uniforms might help the Rocky Road Middle School basketball team, but it was going to take a *lot* more than that to make them look like a real team. For one thing, I think they'd actually have to start making baskets. In fact, getting possession of the ball once or twice might be a good place to start. No offense to Zach, but our basketball team is pretty much a school joke. I've seen them practice — and for all the time the ball spends rolling around on the floor or knocking them on their heads, you would think they were playing soccer.

"Hopefully you'll *play* like a real team, too," Geena commented, obviously agreeing with me. "Watching you guys get killed last week was depressing." It was true. Geena and I had almost died of embarrassment when Green Valley Middle School won 49–0. And those cheer-leaders! They kept taunting us with this incredibly annoying chant the whole game:

> *You can't even catch the ball,*
> *You can't even throw!*
> *Rocky Road should hit the road,*
> *You might as well just go!*

Like I said, incredibly annoying. And totally humil-iating — since, after all, they were right.

"It wasn't our fault!" Zach protested. "With every-body wearing their own clothes, you couldn't tell who was playing and who was watching."

"Oh, so *that's* why you passed the ball to your own mother on her way back from the bathroom?" Geena asked, rolling her eyes.

You probably think she's exaggerating, but here's the bad news: She's not.

Mario laughed at the memory. "Who knew Mrs. Carter-Schwartz had such a good jump shot?" he marveled, still chuckling as he gave us a wave and walked off down the hall.

"Uh, can we get back to what's really important here?" Geena asked, tossing some books inside her locker. "So, picture day. Do I wear my new green tank top to set off my eyes, or will that clash with my new turquoise eye shadow?" She slammed her locker shut in frustration. "How am I ever going to figure all this out in just a couple of days?" she exclaimed, looking at me as if I could supply an answer.

I just shrugged. What did I know about turquoise eye shadow? (Other than the fact that, just maybe, Geena would be better off not wearing it.)

"I don't get it," Zach said, slinging his backpack over his shoulder as we took off down the hall toward the cafeteria. "Why are you so calm about this whole thing?"

"What can I say?" I asked, beaming. "The camera

just loves me. Like, if today were picture day, I'd be fine."

I tossed my hair over my shoulder, and in my imagination, the blondish curtain of silky threads slowly drifted through the air, rippling in the gentle breeze. In reality, my swinging hair whacked into some kid who was passing by, and got stuck in his ID bracelet.

"Aaaah!" I yelped, feeling a sharp tug that almost ripped a chunk of hair out of my head.

"Whoa!" the kid said in surprise, realizing that his hand was now attached to my head.

Wait a second, I recognized that voice. . . . I pushed my hair out of my face and looked up from the hand to the arm, to the shoulder, to the familiar face: *Jake Behari.* Last year's sixth-grade homecoming king. Soccer star. Also known as the crush of my life. For a moment, I just gazed up at him in awe. His head was bent down toward mine as he tried to untangle himself from my hair — his face had never been so close to mine.

"Hey, Singer, how come you can't just say hello like a normal person?" Eli Pataki crowed from somewhere behind Jake. Eli can be such a twerp sometimes. Make that *all* the time. "Oh, I forgot — you're not normal."

He walked off down the hall, his gang of idiots

following close behind and laughing at his dumb joke. I suppose I would have felt a little silly — if it weren't for what happened next.

"Ignore Eli," Jake told me, flashing me a warm grin that made my insides melt and my face burn. "He thinks he's a stand-up comedian."

And it was true. I could still hear Eli doing his stand-up act from halfway down the hall.

But I barely noticed Eli — I was still glowing under the light of Jake's smile. And unless having my hair torn out at the roots had affected my hearing, I was pretty sure he'd actually spoken to me. Jake Behari was trying to reassure me! I mean, I'd only just recently found out that he even knew my name — and now he was actually *talking* to me? As if we were friends or something? *Better think of something clever to say,* I urged myself. I searched furiously for the right words, but nothing useful popped into my head. And the only thing that popped out of my mouth was —

"Ouch!"

"Sorry," Jake mumbled, trying not to tug so hard as he worked to disengage himself from my hair. "Almost got it."

"It's okay," I chirped brightly. "I guess I've just

grown attached to you. Heh-heh." I laughed weakly, cringing inside at the sound of my lame joke. *I guess I've just grown attached to you?* Ugh. What's wrong with me? That was *so* not clever.

Before I had a chance to make myself look like an even bigger loser, Jake finally got my hair out of his bracelet. He pulled his hand away, free and clear, and breathed a sigh of relief. I sighed, too — but for a different reason.

"You can probably get the rest of the hair out with tweezers," I suggested.

No, seriously, *what was wrong with me*? Tweezers? That wasn't cute. That wasn't flirty. That was like something a *teacher* would say. Or maybe the school nurse. Did I really want Jake Behari thinking of me like that? Um, in a word: no.

"All right, later," he said, giving me another smile and walking away down the hall.

I watched him go, amazed as always by his ultra-confident walk. It was like he totally knew how cool he was. But then, in another way, he didn't really know at all. Which somehow made him even cooler. You know?

Talking to Jake had put me into a kind of daze. I just stood there for a moment in the middle of the hall, rubbing the spot on my head where he'd almost yanked my hair out. It was still a little tender.

What a fabulous way to start out the morning.

True, it was awkward and painful.

But still: fabulous.

After school that day, we went to *Juice!*, this juice bar with awesome music and even better smoothies. When my brother, Ben, started working there, I figured that would mean some kind of family discount. But so far, all it means is that I see Ben twice as much as I did before. Which means he's twice as annoying.

I had to wait at the counter for our order to be ready, but Ben was totally ignoring me. What else is new? Instead, he was talking to his friend Marcus. Marcus has been hanging out at our house for years — eating our food, watching our TV, and laughing at all of my brother's stupid jokes. I've known him since he was little. But does he ever remember my name? No way. In fact, I'm not even sure he remembers Ben *has* a sister. Boys are so ridiculous sometimes.

Anyway, like I said, Marcus was talking to Ben. And Ben was . . . "talking" to Marcus.

"Dude, you can't say a word?" Marcus asked him incredulously, widening his eyes in disbelief.

Ben just smiled and then typed something on the laptop that was sitting on the counter between them.

"I bruised my vocal cords singing a heavy metal medley at karaoke," the computer said in this weird robotic monotone.

Ben had done his computer-talk thing for me that morning, so it wasn't a surprise. But still, I thought it was incredibly creepy to hear his words coming out in the computer's voice. Marcus just thought it was cool.

"That stinks," he said. I noticed he was making eye contact with the computer instead of Ben — as if he really thought it had taken on a mind of its own.

Ben typed another sentence on his computer, and a moment later, "Not at all," computer-Ben said. "Watch this."

"Hey, baby," the computer said. "Come here often?"

*Oh, please,* I thought in disgust. *No one would fall for that.*

"Oh my gosh, that's so cool!" a random girl blurted.

She rushed over to the counter and batted her eyes at Ben. "Make it say my name!"

And once again, Ben gets the girl. Not that he even *wants* the girl. He talks a big game, but he's totally in love with his girlfriend, Tara. Unfortunately for him, she moved to California this year. Unfortunately for me, too, since it's all he ever talks about.

I quickly grabbed our smoothies and got out of there, carrying them carefully back to the table. (Sometimes I can be a *little* klutzy. Okay — a *lot* klutzy. But this time I made it back to the table safely, smoothies intact.)

"So, like I was saying," I began as soon as I sat down, picking up our conversation where we'd left off a few minutes ago, "then Jake said that Eli thought he was a stand-up comedian and then —"

"There. Saw it all," Geena cut in, taking a sip from her Berry-ma-taz smoothie. "Back to me — the metallic blue hoops or the yellow chandelier earrings for picture day? Or neither and just a head scarf?"

I sighed. We're back to this? *Again?*

"Just bring 'em all and see how you feel," I suggested wearily.

Geena opened her mouth to respond — and probably to offer us another six options for what shoes she should wear — but before she could, Maris Bingham and

Cranberry St. Clare glided over to our table. Hoping for a change in the topic of conversation, I was almost glad to see them. Don't get me wrong: I said, *almost*. It was Maris and Cranberry, after all. The most popular girls in school (other than Patti Perez, of course). You might think that, to be popular, you had to be *liked* — but I don't know anyone who actually *likes* Maris and Cranberry. Sure, plenty of kids think they're pretty and cool and stylish, but *like* them? That's a different story. Sometimes, I'm not sure they even like each other.

"Speaking of picture day, Addie," Maris said, with her pert nose firmly up in the air, "what are you planning to do about your hair?"

"What do you mean?" I knew I probably should have just ignored her, but I couldn't help myself. "What about my hair?"

"Well, you know." Maris gave her own shiny blond hair a little toss. "It's all . . . flat."

"Especially in pictures," Cranberry pointed out, wrinkling her nose in disgust.

I stopped breathing for a minute, and the world narrowed to a tiny point. All I could see were Maris's and Cranberry's jeering faces. And all I could hear were their voices:

*It's all flat.*
*Especially in pictures.*
*It's all flat.*
*Flat!*
*Flat!*
*Flaaaaaaaaaat!*

I felt ready to crumble into a million tiny pieces. They'd need to sweep me off the floor and throw me into the garbage. I sank down in my chair as low as I could and wished I had the power to disappear. Did I have flat hair? Was I making a fool of myself every time I stepped out in public?

"Know what isn't flat?" Geena asked Maris angrily, stepping up to my defense. "That big zit on your forehead. That'll look pretty on picture day."

I hadn't even noticed the zit until Geena pointed it out, but there it was — scabby and pink, right in the center of Maris's forehead. As she and Cranberry spun on their heels and stalked away, I felt a little better. But not much.

"Forget them, Addie," Geena suggested. "They're so lame."

I knew that. They were lame. Totally, utterly, completely, one hundred percent lame. But . . . were they also right?

*  *  *

I know Geena had told me to forget what Maris and Cranberry said, but I just couldn't. So as soon as I got home, I dug through the hall closet and pulled out a box of old pictures. I was determined to prove Maris and Cranberry wrong. Just one problem with that theory: The pictures didn't look quite how I remembered them. You know how I was saying all that stuff about being totally photogenic and always looking awesome in pictures? Turns out *awesome* wasn't quite the right word — try aw*ful.* Because in every picture, there I was, just like they said: Flat Addie. In photo after photo, my hair looked like it had been painted on my head.

That was it. I could never go out in public again. I was a flat-haired freak!

And the worst part of it all was that I kept hearing Maris's snotty voice echoing through my head.

*It's all flat. Flat hair. Flat hair. Flat. Flat. Flat, flat hair. Flat. Flat.*

I grabbed one of the pictures and threw the rest on the floor. Then I stomped down the hall in search of my mother. How could she have let me out of the house all these years? Much less anywhere near a camera!

I found her sitting at the kitchen table reading a

book. Usually, I'd feel bad about interrupting her, but not this time. I was in full crisis mode.

"Look at my hair!" I cried, slapping the photo down on the table in front of her, as evidence. "This is a disaster!"

"What are you talking about?" Mom asked, closing her book and looking up at me in concern. "You have beautiful hair."

I shook my head. I'd been a kid for long enough to know that it didn't count when she said that kind of thing.

"You have to say that," I pointed out. "You're my mom."

She shook her head and gave me one of those mom looks. It's the same look she gave me in first grade when she told me the tooth fairy was real, despite what Danny Fisher told me on the playground. Let's just say that my mom means well . . . but I've learned not to believe everything that comes out of her mouth.

"I'm saying it because it's true," she insisted. "You know, everyone has something they feel insecure about. Like your father with his toes and me with my teeth." (It's true — my father's totally paranoid about his toes. He never lets anyone see his bare feet — he even wears socks on the beach!) "You just have to focus on all the positive things," Mom continued. "Like your father with his hair and me with my skin." She turned her head from side to side so I could admire her flawless skin. Which . . . okay, it was nice and all, but could we get back to *me* here?

"How am I supposed to focus on the positive?" I asked in despair. "I didn't even know my hair was flat until Maris and Cranberry said so. Now when I look in the mirror, it's all I can see."

"Oh, honey, Maris and Cranberry are just jealous," my mother claimed. "Ignore them. Don't let them get in your head with their monster bringdown."

Uh, *monster bringdown*? Had my mother suddenly been possessed by an MTV veejay from 1998?

"It's an expression I learned from reading my new book on slang," my mother explained enthusiastically when she saw my expression. She held up the book for me to see: *Homes for Homies*. "I'm learning how to talk to young people who are buying their first house. Ya feeling me, G?"

My mom is a real-estate agent, and she's pretty serious about her job. She always claims that if you really want to sell a house, you need to "go that extra mile." Looks like that extra mile took her right into the town square of Weirdsville.

I was about to point that out to her, when Ben came walking into the kitchen, carrying his laptop in one hand and the phone in the other.

"I eat ice cream for dinner." The tinny robotic voice coming out of the computer speakers sounded strange enough in person — I wondered how it sounded through the phone. "Tara. I miss you," the computer said, in an emotionless monotone. "Isn't this cool?"

Okay, so my whole family had bought a one-way ticket to Weirdsville, and it looked like they might be staying for a while. But, really, who was I to judge them? After all, I was the one with the freakishly flat hair. Maybe a house full of weirdos was exactly where I belonged.

I spent that afternoon lying in bed staring at the ceiling, feeling sorry for myself. But it turns out that I wasn't the only one worried about showing my face in public again. While I was suffering through my hair horror, Zach was at basketball practice, about to run into a big problem of his own. Or maybe I should say a *little* problem. Tiny little problem.

See, after practice, the team was finally going to get their new uniforms — just in time to get the team yearbook photo taken on Friday. They could hardly wait. *Finally*, they figured, they'd look like a real team.

"Mario, I should be number thirty-two," Zach was arguing as they horsed around with a Nerf basketball in the locker room. "After all, Zach rhymes with Shaq."

"Zach rhymes with wack, too," Mario pointed out.

"Well, Mario rhymes with mouth, as in 'shut yours,'" Zach retorted as he sank a slam dunk. And then they both stopped short as they saw Coach Pearson walk into the room. And they saw what he was holding.

They were purple shorts with a yellow-and-white stripe across the waistband. And they were small. No, not just small. Teeny. Miniscule. Microscopic. Almost invisible. And Zach had a funny feeling they were about to be his.

The coach, a pale, nervous-looking man who looked like a strong wind might be enough to blow him away, pulled out a box of shorts — all matching the ones he'd held in his hands — and started tossing them to the team. "These are your new uniforms. They're surplus — left over from the seventies. They're all we could afford. Once again." Zach is always complaining about Coach Pearson, and I can see his point. He taught my health class last year and . . . let's just say it doesn't take much to drive him over the edge. Once, when the PA system came on during his class and Principal Brandywine interrupted him with some kind of announcement, I thought his head was going to explode. No, literally. This vein on

25

the side of his neck started throbbing, and his eyes were twitching, and he kept pressing down on his head as if trying to keep something from bursting out. Then things got *really* weird. He started yelling at the PA speaker and asking why it was always trying to ruin his class. Let me say that again, just to be clear. He wasn't yelling at Principal Brandywine, but at the *PA system*. Like he thought it was alive. And out to get him. Coach Pearson doesn't like things to get in his way — which means he *especially* doesn't like Zach.

"Can I get these in a bigger size?" Zach asked foolishly, holding up his shorts. They looked like they would have fit him fine . . . ten years ago.

"Those are extra large," Coach Pearson snapped, with a scary grin. "Shorts were a lot shorter in the seventies — any more complaints and you'll get a small."

Coach Pearson and the rest of the team started laughing at the thought of it and, after a moment, so did Zach. But then, abruptly, Coach Pearson fell silent and wiped the smile off his face. He shot Zach a deadly glare.

"Not kidding."

If I'd only known about Zach's "tiny" problem, maybe I wouldn't have felt so alone. But instead, by that night, I was feeling like I didn't have a friend in the world. At least, not one who could understand what I was going through. Geena had gorgeous hair — curly and bouncy and filled with body, just like a shampoo model. Zach was a boy, so what did he care? And my mom had certainly been no help, with her momlike compliments and perfect complexion. I looked down to the foot of my bed, where my dog, Nancy, had curled up on my quilt to nap. Even *Nancy* had better hair than me — it was all golden and fluffy. No, I was all alone with this one.

I knew it wasn't that important — I knew I should just ignore what Maris and Cranberry had said. But knowing that didn't make it any easier to do it. So, instead, I grabbed my guitar. When I'm feeling this low, there's only one thing that helps — writing a song.

> *Don't know what happened to me today,*
> *Why I'm suddenly carin' what them girls say.*
> *Mama says don't sweat it — them girls are just mean.*
> *But Mama don't get it — she ain't thirteen.*
> *I'm singing the flat-hair insecurity blues.*
> *My life is trash. Trash. My life is trash.*

Somehow, it didn't make me feel any better.

4

I ran into Zach at our lockers the next morning, and as soon as he spotted me, he whipped out his new uniform to show me.

"Can you believe we have to wear these in front of people?" he asked in a desperate-sounding voice. "I couldn't even look at myself in the mirror last night!"

On another morning, I might have laughed at the thought of Zach parading around in minishorts, and then come up with something supercomforting to tell him, like how no one would notice. (Even though it wouldn't be quite true, it would be nice for him to hear.) But that morning, I was just too consumed with my own problems. Flat, flat, flat, flat hair was still all I could think about.

Fortunately, I was saved from having to come up with anything to say. Because suddenly, Geena rushed up to us and shoved a giant photograph in our faces. It was a picture of her — and she looked . . .

"Amazing!" I gushed. It was a glamour shot that made Geena look like a movie star.

"When did you have this taken?" Zach asked in awe.

"I didn't!" Geena said exuberantly. She was practically bouncing up and down. "Julian made it!"

"Is that a secret girl thing?" Zach asked, crinkling his face in confusion. "'Cause I don't know what that means."

"Julian's this guy in the art lab. He can create a whole bunch of different looks for you on his computer. Now I know that 'hair down' totally works for me. He's a genius."

"And some kind of magician, too, if you know what I'm saying," Zach commented, gesturing toward Geena's body in the picture.

"Well, we did put my head on a fashion model's body," Geena admitted, "but that's cool. I mean, we are similar body types. Addie, you should —"

But I didn't even wait for her to get the words out of her mouth. Geena was absolutely right: Julian was the answer to all my problems. I left her in mid-sentence, racing off down the hall in search of my flat-hair salvation.

Julian had set up shop in the art lab — and he'd gotten some sixth-grade artsy wannabe to guard the door. As I skidded to a halt in front of the doorway, she held up an arm to block me from going in, then held out a gray plastic tray. You know, the kind they have in airports when you're going through the metal detectors? I just stared at her — what did I need with a tray? I just needed Julian!

"Please remove all jewelry," she commanded, in a voice that sounded strangely like Ben's computer. "Necklaces, rings, wristwatches."

I shrugged my shoulders and did as I was told, depositing my charm necklace, my earrings, and all my rings and bracelets into the plastic tray.

"Julian will see you now," the artsy girl told me, taking me to the back of the room. Julian, whose black clothes matched his dark hair and darker expression, sat in front of a computer, staring at the giant screen.

"It's great to meet you — I'm a huge fan of your work," I babbled. He didn't even look up. But he had to be listening. Right? "I saw what you did for my friend Geena Fabiano? She looked great —"

I stopped in surprise, blinded by the flash as Julian's assistant snapped a picture of me. I wasn't ready,

I wasn't even smiling, but, well, Julian had to know what he was doing. Right?

"So, um, I was wondering if you could help me with my hair?" I continued as the bright spots from the flash faded away. "I was thinking more of a —"

"Silence!" the girl ordered me, handing Julian the camera so he could hook it up to his computer. "He doesn't like chatter."

Was it just me or was this getting stranger by the minute?

I shrugged and walked over to the computer screen so I could see what he was looking at. It was me! Or rather, my face, with a bunch of other people's hair.

"Okay, let's see," Julian mumbled, clicking through the options. "I've got the punk rock."

My head topped by two feet of platinum spikes? Hmm — I don't think so.

"Next."

My face on the screen peeked out from behind the Elvira threads of an eighties rock star. Was that look *ever* cool? Somehow, I doubted it.

"The hip-hop."

Ever imagined what you'd look like as a hard-core rapper with sticklike dreads poking out all over your head? Let's just say . . . not really the look I was going for.

"The supermodel."

Bingo. There I was on the screen with long wavy hair. And I looked fabulous. It was as far from flat as you could get. This was it, the new me. I just knew it.

Julian printed out the picture for me. I just couldn't stop staring at it. And I definitely couldn't wait to get home that afternoon so I could get started on my total hair makeover!

My hair makeover was totally intense. I spent hours crimping, curling, cajoling, everything I could think to do to whip it into shape. My desk, bureau, and bed were covered with supplies — two curling irons, six combs and four brushes, a hair dryer, three kinds of gel — I was as prepared as could be.

And I didn't mind a little hard work. In fact, I didn't even notice it. I was too excited about my new look. I couldn't stop myself from dancing around the room as I crimped and curled, singing my newest song, "Good-bye to Flat Hair."

*Look at me now.*
*Hey! Look at me now.*
*Good-bye, stringy — hello, springy,*
*Hello, hair so great.*

*Ready for the yearbook,*
*Bring in my new look.*
*Hey! Look at me now!*
*Hey! Look at me now!*

And finally, finally, finally, I was ready to look at myself in the mirror. The new, supermodel-ified me.

Uh-oh.

Let's just say that when I saw what I'd done to myself, I screamed so loud, I woke up my grandmother from her nap. And she was napping three hundred miles away.

I know you probably want to hear more about my hair and what it actually looked like, but . . . it's just too traumatic. I need a moment to recover from the memory of that horror, and then, I promise, I'll tell all. But in the meantime, just so you don't get bored while you're waiting, let's check in and see how Zach was dealing with his own makeover. Because the day after I destroyed my hair, he had basketball practice. And that meant it was time for the new uniforms. The team gathered around the coach's desk, looking like they'd been attacked by the seventies. From the waist up, their uniforms looked totally normal: loose purple tank tops, each emblazoned with a giant yellow number. But from the waist down? That was another story . . . after all, short-shorts went out of style in the seventies for a reason. And no thirteen-year-old guy should *ever* have to show that much leg.

"I hate whiny babies," the coach finally snapped, tired of listening to all the complaining. "You know, I wore those very shorts when I played for Rocky Road back in seventy-eight!" He handed Zach a framed photo from the edge of his desk, and the team crowded in to get a good look. There was Coach Pearson in his white knee socks and short-shorts, accepting a giant trophy.

"How come that guy next to you isn't wearing these shorts?" Zach asked, pointing to a figure in long blue shorts and a white shirt, handing Coach Pearson the trophy.

"What guy?" Coach Pearson scowled up at Zach. "That's Principal Brandywine! She used to be Coach Brandywine back then!"

Oops. The guys on the team all recoiled in horror. It was hard to know what to be more revolted by: the thought of our ancient principal running around the court in her headband and athletic shorts, or the thought of going out in public looking like the 1978 version of Coach Pearson.

"Enough chitty-chat," the coach grouched. "Let's get moving. Everybody grab a —" He stopped suddenly, realizing the bag of basketballs that should have been sitting next to his desk was, in fact, nowhere in sight. "Darn it! I left the ball bag in the car." There went that throbbing vein again. And his eyes had started bulging. The team stepped back, not wanting to get spattered if he actually blew up this time. "You know I hate that we can't afford our own balls! And that we have to borrow them from the Senior Center every week! And that my wife left me for her boss!"

There was dead silence.

"Okay, Zach, go to my car and get the ball bag from the trunk." He tossed Zach a set of keys.

"But that's all the way in the parking lot!" Zach said, his voice filling with desperation. He looked down at his basketball uniform. "I have to go through the whole school to get there!"

The coach glared at him. It was a dangerous glare, an if-looks-could-kill-we'd-be-making-you-a-coffin glare.

"You know what I hate right now?" the coach asked.

Zach swallowed hard. "Me?" he asked in a tiny voice.

"Bingo."

Zach snuck through the halls of the school, delirious with relief that they were pretty much empty. He paused at the end of one hall, hiding himself behind a bank of lockers, and peered around the corner. Only one more long hallway standing between him and the parking lot. He could totally do this. He crept around the corner and began to hurry down the hall — just as the entire girls' volleyball team swept by.

There were about ten girls, all dressed in their own Rocky Road uniforms. They looked just like Zach's — except that their uniforms actually fit.

"Nice short-shorts," the team captain called out.

Eyes wide with horror and shame, Zach sped up, trying to get away.

"Hey, baby, where're you going in such a hurry?" the captain cried.

Enough was enough. Zach slipped inside the next doorway he came to and slammed the door shut behind him. No way was he ever leaving that room again.

He took a deep breath, savoring the moment of peace and quiet — and then realized that he wasn't alone.

"Nice hot pants!" Geena cackled. We both stared at his outfit in shock. I mean, he'd already shown us the uniform — but seeing him hold up the minishorts was a whole different thing from seeing him *wear* them.

"What are you doing in here?" Zach asked, totally confused.

"What are *you* doing in here?" I countered. I wasn't

quite ready to explain why it was that I'd dragged Geena into this empty classroom to deal with my crisis.

"I'm escaping a mob of girls!" Zach exclaimed. "They made me feel like a piece of meat. I've never been so humiliated in my life." He hung his head.

"At least you can take the shorts off and be normal," I reassured him dejectedly. "I'm gonna have to wear a hat for the rest of my life!"

I had stuffed all my hair under a giant hat so that no one in school would see what had happened. But these were my two best friends in the world, right? I was counting on them to help me fix this — which meant that, first, I was going to have to show them what had happened.

I took a deep breath.

Then another.

Then I slowly pulled off the hat.

Zach's eyes widened.

"Dude," he gasped, taking a step backward.

"Wow." Geena put a hand to her own hair, as if to reassure herself it was still intact. "You look like . . . Little Orphan Annie."

And, sad to say, it was true. My hair looked like I had stuck my finger in a light socket. I'd crimped it, blow-dried it, and singed it beyond recognition. It was totally fried. I could just see myself dressed up as Annie, all alone on a big, dark stage, singing out my misery at the top of my lungs:

*Tomorrow morning I'll be closing the door,*
*No one will ever see me anymore,*
*Or I'll run away — 'cause it's picture day,*
*And I look like some freak on a Broadway stage.*
*Picture day, tomorrow,*
*It's picture day, tomorrow . . .*

My friends' faces told me that I looked even worse than I'd thought. With a sigh, I pulled my hat back on, tucking the brittle, dry mop of hair underneath as best I could.

"Why's it red?" Geena finally asked, breaking the silence.

"After I crimped it to death, I tried fixing it with henna," I explained, shivering at the memory of that horrible decision. "But I guess I left it in too long. *What am I gonna do?*" I cried, desperate for their help. "Picture day is tomorrow!"

"Only one thing you can do," Zach responded, shaking his head at the hopelessness of the situation. "Shave it off. Shave it *all* off."

"Thanks for the advice," I snapped. No way was I trading in my horrible Annie 'do for an even worse Daddy Warbucks chrome dome. "I guess I have no choice," I continued in a softer voice. I was resigned to my fate. "I'm gonna cut picture day and take the haiku."

So what if I'd never cut a day of school before in my life?

And so what if the next time my grandmother wanted to show her grandchildren off to her friends, all she would have is a framed photo of Ben and a framed haiku. (I could just hear her friends from the canasta club now: "He's very handsome — but her poem doesn't rhyme.")

"I think you fried more than your hair," Geena remarked, rolling her eyes. "Are you forgetting about Principal Brandywine?"

"Yeah, if you're not here, she'll call your house," Zach reminded me. "She lives for this kind of thing."

"Don't worry," I assured him. "I've got that all figured out."

And it was true. On my long list of worries, getting past Principal Brandywine was way down at the bottom. After all, I might not have much experience with getting in and out of this kind of trouble — but I knew someone who did. . . .

*Sometimes having a big brother is a good thing,* I thought to myself as Ben got his computerized-voice thing all set up. Not that I would ever say it out loud to him, but there are times when a big brother is exactly what you need. This, as it turned out, was one of those times.

Ben gave me a thumbs-up, and I picked up the phone and dialed the number. I held it up to the computer speaker as he typed — and leaned in to listen to the voice on the other end.

"Brandywine." She answered on the second ring.

"Hello, Principal Brandywine." Ben's computer-generated mom voice sounded like . . . well, like a computer-generated mom voice. I could only hope it would get the job done. "This is Mrs. Singer."

"Oh, hello, Mrs. Singer," Principal Brandywine said. Excellent — she'd bought it! "How nice to hear from —"

"Addie will not be at school today, as she is sick."

"Oh, I'm so sorry to hear —"

"Please join me for tea sometime." I glared at Ben, gesturing wildly to try to get him to stop cutting off the principal before she could finish a sentence.

"I'd love to —"

"Good-bye," he typed, and grabbed the phone from me, hanging it up.

Okay, so it wasn't done with much grace or subtlety, but it was done. Of course, I would have to clean Ben's room for the next few months, but at least I'd have some help. Zach decided to cut picture day, too. He said there was no way he'd be in the basketball team picture if he had to reveal so much of his body. (And after seeing him in his short-shorts, I couldn't blame him.)

Zach handed me Coach Pearson's phone number, and I dialed it for Ben, holding the phone up to the computer again.

"Hello, Coach Pearson," the computer bleated robotically. "This is Mr. Schwartz. Zach will not be at practice today, as he is dead."

Have I mentioned that my big brother, Ben, is a

world-class idiot? I smacked him on the arm, but he just grinned up at me and kept typing.

"Please join me for tea sometime. Good-bye."

Zach and I needed somewhere to lay low until school was out, and we figured *Juice!* would be our best bet. It's usually almost empty during the day — just slackers and writers. (And, come on, is there really a difference?) Nobody we know goes there until after school. So Zach and I crept furtively through the neighborhood. I kept checking over my shoulder, afraid we'd be spotted. But every time, the coast was clear. Still, I felt like someone was watching us. Maybe it was because I was totally paranoid about getting caught. Or maybe it was because, even though it was a beautiful sunny day, Zach and I were both bundled up in heavy hooded sweatshirts. We were trying to stay incognito.

Believe me, I felt really bad about having to lie and cut school. But I just couldn't risk everyone seeing me when I looked like Bozo the Clown. We finally made it to *Juice!* and exchanged a glance of relief before opening the door. As we stepped inside, I let out a loud gasp — and next to me, Zach almost fell over in shock. Because *Juice!* wasn't empty. Not by a long shot. Sure, there were a few of the usual slackers, slumped over their laptops. But they weren't the only ones.

I'd never seen *Juice!* so full. It looked like the entire student body was packed inside.

"Addie! Zach!" Geena cried with joy, spotting us through the crowd and pushing her way through toward us.

"Geena, what are you doing here?" I asked in confusion. Wasn't she the one who told me I'd never get away with cutting school?

"What is *everybody* doing here?" Zach added, gesturing toward the counter, where the entire basketball team was ordering drinks.

"Cutting picture day!" Geena replied, as if it should have been totally obvious. (And I guess it should've been.) "I tried on everything in my closet this morning, and nothing looked as good as my model picture that Julian made," she confided. "So I gave up." Then Geena grabbed a piece of paper from her table. "I'm writing my haiku — wanna hear it so far?"

Uh, no, not really — but did I have a choice?

Apparently not.

"Bird in a dead tree," Geena intoned, counting the syllables on her fingers as she went. "Your sad song calling to me. Tweet, tweet, tweet. Tweet, tweet." She stopped and looked up at us expectantly. "So, what do you think?"

"I don't get it," Zach admitted.

Geena laughed and tossed the paper back on the table. "Yeah, me neither. But it has the right amount of syllables."

I still couldn't believe that the entire school had ducked out of picture day. I even spotted Maris and Cranberry at a nearby table, complaining to some of their friends.

"Normally, I have such perfect skin," Maris whimpered, keeping one hand plastered over the angry red pimple on her forehead. "I couldn't possibly have my picture taken with this giant zit!"

"I hear that," Cranberry put in, shaking her head in disgust. "I'm retaining so much water, the name under my picture would be Bloat-berry St. Clare!"

Who knew that even Maris and Cranberry worried about looking bad? I didn't think Maris and Cranberry worried about anything, other than which of their parents' credit cards to borrow for their latest shopping spree.

But even that wasn't the biggest surprise. And though I was amazed to spot Jake Behari, of all people, that wasn't the biggest surprise, either. No, the biggest shock of all came a moment later, when Jake came up to talk to me. That's right, Jake Behari came all the way across the café to *talk to me.*

"Hey, Addie," he said with an easy grin.

"Jake?" I asked, wishing I could pinch myself to make sure this wasn't a dream. (Unfortunately, that might have looked a little odd.) Normally, I freeze up whenever Jake is around, but this time, I was so surprised and confused that the words just came pouring out. Maybe that wasn't such a good thing. "What're you doing here? You're, like, perfect." My heart skipped a beat as I realized what I had just said. What if he figured out that I *liked* him — it would be so humiliating! "I mean, you know . . ."

"Thanks," he said with a laugh, saving me from floundering around for something to explain myself. I could feel my cheeks heating up. I just knew they had flushed bright red. *So* embarrassing. "I just came to drag my buds back to school," he explained. "What're you doing here?"

"Oh, uh, I had a sort of hair-related mishap." Now, why had I said that? Why couldn't I stop myself from saying all these things that would make him think I was an idiot? "See, my hair is so flat, I thought I'd curl it, but that didn't work, so I thought henna — but hello, worse — so I came here. . . ."

*Earth to Addie, stop talking! Just — STOP.*

"Huh. Well, I like your hair the way it normally is," Jake told me. Jake Behari had noticed my hair? And he liked it! I couldn't stop myself from grinning. "I mean, when it's not caught in my bracelet."

This was so crazy. It was like Jake and I were having, like, a normal conversation. Suddenly, he leaned his head in close to mine, and I almost stopped breathing. This was the second time in a week that our faces had been so close together. What was he doing? Was he going to —

"By the way," he whispered, "I'm not perfect. Have you seen my ears?"

Talking to Jake made me realize something: Mom was right. (I guess there's a first time for everything.) Everyone has something they feel insecure about. Even someone as perfect-seeming as Jake Behari. And that's why I decided to do it. Go back to school and get my picture taken. Geena and Zach didn't understand at first — but they came along. Because that's what best friends do.

I think I finally figured something out: The trick is to focus on the positive and not let your insecurities keep you from doing the things you love. Like, in my case, getting my picture taken. When we got back to school and found the yearbook photographer, we discovered that only a few other students had had the nerve to show up. So we didn't have long to wait for our moment in the spotlight.

Geena went first, and she only complained a little about not having time to reapply her makeup. She decided that even if she doesn't look like a superstar, she would still have the best-looking picture of last names F through H. Next up was Zach, wearing his retro uniform. It was supposed to be a picture of the entire team, but Zach was the only player who had the nerve to show up.

I was a little worried that he might lose his nerve when some of those volleyball girls started whistling at him again — but I underestimated Zach. This time, instead of blushing and running away, he stopped in his tracks and turned around to face them.

"How would you feel if someone treated your brother that way?" he asked, his voice loud and clear, and filled with righteous anger. "I will *not* allow you to objectify me. There's more to Zach Carter-Schwartz than looking good in shorts."

Watching him made me so proud. And it gave me the confidence I needed to get in front of the camera myself. Feeling less nervous than I expected, I pulled off my hat. I could feel my bright red, dry, frizzy mess of hair spring away from my head. I smiled as the flash-bulb went off — and the smile was real, just like the rest of me. I might not be perfect, I decided, but maybe that was okay. Because I'd rather just be *me*.

So I got in a little bit of trouble for the whole cutting-school thing — grounded for a week, with no phone privileges.

"Chill, peeps, chill," Mom said as she was walking past my bedroom on the phone with one of her clients. I guess she was still practicing her *Homes for Homies* slang. "I'll blow up your celly with the 411 and . . . Oh, hold on a sec—" She clicked over to the call-waiting. "Hello? I'm sorry, Geena, no — Addie can*not* come to the phone."

I also had to be my brother's personal slave for a while, to pay him back for getting me out of school. You have no idea how irritating it is to be ordered around by someone's computer. But you know what? I'm still glad the whole thing happened — and I'm especially glad that I went back to have my picture taken. Because no matter how complicated things get, it's nice to know there are some people who will always think you're fabulous. (Even if those people are mainly your grandparents.)

Besides, all those days stuck in my room gave me plenty of time to write another song:

*There's a truth that will set you free.*
*Everybody's freaked out, not just me.*
*It could be your hair, it could be your nose,*
*You could look like a dork in gym clothes.*
*Be yourself, that's what you gotta do,*
*Or you could end up with a bad haiku.*
*Tweet, tweet, tweet. Tweet, tweet . . .*
*The bird is dead.*

Like I said, I was grounded for a week — and by the time my sentence was lifted, my hair (with the help of loads of conditioner) had finally gone back to normal. I had never been so happy to see flat hair in my entire life. That was the good news. The bad news? My grounding ended on the same day our mother-daughter book club was supposed to meet at our house. I was hoping that maybe at the last minute, my mom would decide to extend my punishment for a day and cancel the book club. But no such luck — she said I'd served my time and I deserved a little treat. She didn't realize that the *real* treat would have been if she'd canceled book club. For good.

My mom signed us up for the club a couple of months ago, as a fun way to learn and to spend time together. She called it "infotainment." I call it "boring."

Every week, we met at a different person's house and sat around talking about some lame book that I'd barely been able to read without falling asleep. And it's not like any of *my* friends were in the group. No, there was basically nothing fun about it whatsoever. Except for my mom's stuffed mushroom caps, my favorite appetizer. I popped one in my mouth every minute or so, trying to stay awake. It was barely working.

"I thought it was wonderful when the tears flowed from Lindsay's eyes and landed on her lilacs," one mother commented, pantomiming tears running down her face.

The woman sitting across from me, dressed in a pink preppy blazer and a string of pearls, nodded sagely.

"The purple lilacs represent Lindsay's fear of rejection," she declared.

Mom grinned. She loves it when people start talking about symbolism and all that stuff — she says it reminds her of college.

"That's very insightful, Karen."

"It's *Kahr*-ren," the woman corrected her in a snotty voice.

"Of course." Mom smiled at her through gritted teeth. "Addie, any thoughts?"

*But I had finally lost my battle against sleep. I pitched forward and did a nosedive into the plate of mushroom caps and mini pizzas. The plate flipped over and sent a hail of mushroom caps flying through the room. Mothers and daughters shrieked and ducked for cover.*

"Addie!" my mother repeated loudly, waking me from my little fantasy. I liked the fantasy better. I picked up the copy of this week's book, *Lilacs for Lindsay,* and searched for something to say. It was a little hard. . . . I'd only read halfway through before giving up and turning back to *Star Style* magazine. Suddenly, I noticed the author's photo on the back, this gray-haired guy in a flowered turtleneck and earrings. It was totally weird — and it gave me a brilliant idea.

"Uh, well, I think it's cool that a book with so many female characters was written by a guy," I finally said, feeling pretty good about myself. It seemed like an extremely sophisticated and insightful point to make . . . especially for someone who hadn't read the book.

Mom shook her head and looked disappointed.

"Addie," she said sadly, "that's a woman. It's Dr. *Eleanor* Mezzrow."

"Oh." Well, how was I supposed to know? I mean,

look at that picture — no *way* was that a woman. "Really? I thought, you know, 'cause of the mustache . . ."

An awkward silence settled over the room, and the women and their daughters all just sat there and stared at me. What were they waiting for me to say? I had no idea, so I did the only thing I could think of. I started stuffing my face with Mom's mini pizzas.

"Did I say how good these mini pizzas are?" I asked around a mouthful of cheesy goodness.

"Yes, honey, eight times," Mom reminded me. "Now, what are your thoughts about *Lilacs for Lindsay*?"

*I think it's a boring book about a boring girl and her boring flowers?*

No, it didn't seem like that would go over very well.

Just as I was about to admit that I didn't know anything about the book — that I hadn't even read the book — my cell phone rang. Saved by the bell!

Shooting an apologetic glance at our guests, I flipped open my little pink phone, and Geena's name flashed up on the caller ID. *Perfect.*

"Geena!" I cried eagerly into the phone.

"Hey, I just painted my nails and I have six-point-two minutes before they dry properly and I move on to my toes, so I'm good for a chat."

"He crashed into *what*?" I said loudly, trying to sound horrified. I widened my eyes and turned down the corners of my mouth to make my face look as distraught as I could. "That's horrible!"

"You're using me as an excuse to get away from those book moms, aren't you?" Oh, like she'd never used *me* as a phone excuse before. What else were best friends for?

"Don't cry, Geena," I urged her, in a fake comforting tone. "Don't cry. We'll get through this together."

"Ooooh, nice touch," Geena complimented me. I barely heard her — I was on a mission. An escape mission.

"I have to take this," I silently mouthed to my mother. She nodded sympathetically and motioned for me to go ahead. I got up and threaded my way through the group to head upstairs — a clean getaway.

As I was heading toward my bedroom, I could hear my mother wrapping things up.

"Well, that's it. Don't forget, next week, the book club will meet at Kahr-ren and Brenda's house."

"It's *Breen*-da," Kahr-ren's daughter said.

"Of course," Mom said. "*Breen*-da." And even though I couldn't see her from the stairway, I could picture the expression on her face: perfectly sweet and composed, but with gritted teeth behind her smile and a sliver of ice in her eyes. Mom was too polite to ever say anything, but I suspected she felt exactly the same way about those two as I did.

I ran up the rest of the stairs and slipped into my bedroom, throwing myself down onto the bed.

"Addie, why do you stay in that book club if you hate it?" Geena asked — and not for the first time.

"What am I supposed to do?" I countered. "I can't just tell my mom I hate it. She'll be so —"

A piercing beeping noise blasted through the phone. I winced and held it away from my ear.

"Oops, gotta go," Geena said, once the noise had stopped. "It's toe time."

She hung up before I even had a chance to say good-bye. I flipped the phone shut in irritation and checked my watch. That was *so* not six-point-two minutes.

I thought about it all afternoon, and by dinnertime, I had come to a decision: I just had to do the mature, grown-up thing . . . and avoid telling Mom the truth until the day I die. And maybe if I played my cards right, I wouldn't have to tell her the truth. Maybe I could just help her figure it out on her own.

So, as I helped her make dinner that night, I did

my best to sound totally unenthused about book club — which wasn't too hard.

"What'd you think of those mushroom caps I made for book club?" she asked, stirring a pot over the stove.

"Fine," I told her, and focused on washing the lettuce.

"Because we could always try another recipe," Mom suggested.

I just shrugged. Telling her that the mushroom caps were delicious didn't seem like it really fit with my plan.

"You know, Addie, *you* could make something for book club," my dad suggested. He was over at the dining room table, slicing some bread. He may have been helping with dinner, but he definitely wasn't helping my cause. "Maybe your famous walnut crescents?"

Uh-oh. I knew what was coming next.

"Oh!" Mom said, lighting up at the idea. "We could go see Nut Jim. I know how you love it when he cracks nuts on your head."

Um, okay, about Nut Jim. He's this crazy old man in a plaid shirt and overalls who runs a nut stand down in the town square. His big gimmick is that, if you want, he'll crack walnuts on your head.

Now, when I was a kid, I thought this was just a fabulous idea. He'd crack a walnut on my head, and I'd giggle and clap, and cry, "More, Nut Jim! More!"

But here's the thing. The older I got, the more I began to understand: Having someone crack walnuts on your head? Actually, not so much fun. Plus, it kind of hurts. And I can only imagine how humiliating it would be if anyone from school actually saw me.

But I could never tell Mom that — it would hurt her feelings. She loved taking me to Nut Jim. So every time we needed to buy nuts, away we went to Nut Jim. And as soon as he saw me, he'd grin, pull out a walnut, and —

CRACK!

Right on my head. These days, my mom was the only one who giggled and jumped up and down, crying, "More, Nut Jim! More!" (Easy for her to say — it wasn't *her* head.) She never seemed to notice that the whole thing made me miserable.

*Enough is enough,* I thought, tearing angrily at the lettuce. Maybe I should just tell her the truth. "You know, Mom, I don't think —" And then I saw the look on her face. It was so . . . sad. I reminded myself that parents can be very fragile people. Sometimes, you've got to make some sacrifices for them. "— that we should use nuts," I finished lamely. "Um, Breen-da has a major nut allergy," I lied, thinking fast. "She'll die."

Mom gasped in horror, accidentally dropping her spoon into the bubbling pot of sauce. "I was this close to putting pine nuts in the mushroom caps!" she exclaimed. "I'll leave myself a reminder message." She whipped out her cell phone and pressed a button. "Remember, no nuts," she told her future self. "Breen-da will die."

She went back to stirring her pot — and I went back to trying to be the perfect, dutiful, book-club-loving daughter.

Fortunately, Ben saved me from having to come up with any more lies. (Like I said, sometimes big brothers come in handy.)

He breezed into the living room, fresh from taking his learner's permit test, and Dad leaped to his feet, eager to hear what had happened.

"There's the champ!" he cheered. "So, how'd your test go?"

Ben flashed him a thumbs-up and whipped out a piece of paper. "Let's just say I had an *ace* up my sleeve," he crowed. (He'd gotten his voice back, so no more computer-generated speech.) "You know, 'cause I *aced* it? Eh? Eh?"

Yes, Ben, we all got your joke — we just didn't think it was funny.

He waved the paper in the air. "Learner's permit!" he cried, sliding it back into his pocket.

"That's great!" Dad enthused, slapping him on the back. "Car's all gassed up and ready for your first driving lesson."

"Dad, hold up," Ben cautioned. "I want to learn on Mom's car."

I couldn't believe he was being so picky. Do you know what I would give to drive *any* car? Three years is *so* long to wait.

"Is it because of the smell in my car?" Dad asked, looking a little embarrassed. "Because it's not really vomit — someone spilled a latte and it went bad. . . ."

"It's not the smell. Mom's car is a stick shift," Ben explained, mimicking shifting gears. "Girls dig guys that can drive stick."

Oh, please.

He pretended he was shifting gears again and driving away across the living room. Then, with a sudden screech, he skidded to a halt and pounded on his nonexistent horn. "Come on!" he shouted. Then he turned toward us to explain, "I'm stuck behind a garbage truck."

Does Ben think girls also dig guys who still play Let's Pretend?

No wonder his girlfriend moved three thousand miles away.

I was feeling pretty good about my whole "grin and bear it" plan when it came to mother-daughter bonding. After all, what my mother didn't know couldn't hurt her, right? And as long as I played along as the model daughter a few times a week, she'd never have to know that I thought all this stuff was lame. It would be like living a double life. With Mom, I'd be "good little Addie" who still loved Nut Jim and tea parties, but when she wasn't around, I'd break out my secret identity, "fabulous teen Addie," who was (almost) all grown up. It'd be like being a superhero — only without the cape and tights.

Except here's the thing: turns out the whole secret-identity, double-life thing is a little harder than it looks. Because what are you supposed to do when both your lives are happening at the same time? I had no idea — but I was about to find out.

"So, are we all on for *Juice!* tonight?" Geena asked the next morning at school. We were on our way to math, to take a test I totally wasn't ready for. I was so busy worrying that, at first, I barely heard Geena. But then I realized what she had said — and it wiped all thoughts of variables and exponents out of my mind.

"I can't," I confessed, chewing on the inside of my cheek. I'd forgotten all about our plans to go to *Juice!* "I told my mom I'd go shopping with her," I explained. I wondered if I sounded a little bitter. (After all, I felt it.) "I didn't mean to, but she ambushed me with the promise of new jeans."

"You know that jeans are made by toddlers in sweatshops," Zach pointed out.

Gee, Zach, thanks for the public service announcement.

"*All* jeans?" Geena asked, peering at him suspiciously. I could hear the doubt in her voice.

But he just ignored her and proudly pointed to his baggy beige pants. "These burlap pants were made by the Amish out of potato sacks," he told us, beaming.

I stifled a giggle, and Geena rolled her eyes. Zach didn't even notice — he was too busy admiring his pants.

"Addie, if we don't put in more hours at *Juice!,* we'll never get invited to The Point," Geena reminded me.

"The Point?" I repeated in a hushed voice. Suddenly, I had a vision of Geena and me at The Point, doing . . . well, nobody really knows *what* happens at The Point. All the coolest high school kids hang out there, and they do whatever it is cool high school kids do. It's so cool, and so top secret, that you can't go unless someone invites you. And — I sighed at the thought — who would invite me? "I've been begging Ben to take me there for a year," I complained. It was true. Over the summer, I asked him almost every day. And every day, he just laughed in my face.

"We're not just gonna get invited by some random at *Juice!,*" I scoffed to Geena.

Zach grimaced — he hates it when Geena and I gossip about The Point. Which we do, oh, every five minutes or so.

"Who cares?" he grouched. "I hear that place is full of poseurs and future white-collar criminals."

Seriously, Zach just didn't get it.

"It's also full of high school kids," I pointed out to him, in the same tone my mother uses when she has to remind me, for the hundredth time, to hang my wet towel up after I'm done with it. "Everything cool that's happened has happened at The Point."

And I'm talking, like, everything cool that's happened *ever*.

"I heard that was where Janette Sperling wore the first mini backpack in 1992," Geena gushed.

Zach rolled his eyes in disbelief, but Geena just ignored him.

"According to *Yes!* magazine, the reason we haven't been invited there is 'cause we've been sending out hostile vibes with our body language," Geena said, sounding very businesslike and determined. She had the can-do look in her eye — and when Geena's determined to get something, she usually does. On the other hand . . . "hostile vibes with our body language"?

I gave her a skeptical look.

"That's exactly what I'm talking about," Geena said triumphantly, gesturing toward me. I looked down at myself — arms crossed, shoulders hunched. I guess it *could* be seen as hostile. Sort of? "You want to get invited to The Point," Geena continued, "you need to have an easy smile and never touch your nose. Work on that for tonight."

I whipped my hand away from my face, hoping no

one had spotted me scratching my nose, then shook my head.

"I can't blow off my mom to go to *Juice!*" I reminded her. Besides, I reminded myself, what did Geena really know about getting invited to The Point? I mean, she talked like she had all the answers. But if she really did, wouldn't she have gotten invited already? On the other hand, every once in a while, Geena was actually right about something like this. Maybe I could just tell my mom I didn't want to hang out with her. . . .

*My mother lay in her hospital bed, head lolling weakly against the pillows. The doctor flicked her latest X-rays onto his light board and frowned. Ben, Dad, and I waited anxiously to hear what the doctor would say.*

*The doctor turned to us and shook his head sadly.*

*"I'm sorry, her condition is worse," he told us, holding up one of the X-rays.*

*"It's her heart. . . . It's broken."*

*They all turned to stare at me, and I could feel the accusation in their eyes.*

*What? Just because I'd told my mom I didn't want to hang out with her, and reduced her to a sobbing heap*

*in a hospital bed? Just because I'd broken her heart, was
I supposed to feel guilty forever?*

*Yes.* My new song said it all:

*Broke my mother's heart in two,
I feel like a selfish shrew.*

"So? Tell her the truth," Zach urged me, knocking
me out of the daydream. "Your mom's cool. She'll understand."

But would she? I wanted to believe him, I did. But
I just kept imagining that X-ray of her broken heart — and
I knew the crushed look on her face would be even worse.

"Addie, we can't waste our youth doing boring things," Geena warned me, "or we'll turn into
boring people."

I had to admit, it was a valid point. And my mom
would never want me to be boring, right? She was
always saying how she just wanted the best for me. So
wouldn't she *want* me to take advantage of my youth?
Wouldn't she hate for me to throw it all away, just for
some mother-daughter mall time?

"You're right!" I suddenly said, feeling like a dark
cloud over my head had just evaporated.

"Who's right, Geena or me?" Zach asked in confusion. "Because they're two distinct points of view."

"I can't waste my time worrying about my mom," I told them both confidently. Although I sounded more confident than I felt. Inside, I was thinking about my song lyrics.

Geena smiled, thrilled that I'd taken her advice. She made a "score one for me" notch in the air — Zach just sulked. But none of that was really important. The important thing was that I suddenly realized a major truth about life. Yes, sometimes it's good to think of other people's feelings — but sometimes, you just have to think about yourself. And this definitely seemed like one of those times.

"Mom gets to do what she wants, and I should get to do what I want," I said, getting more certain with every passing second. "And I want to go to The Point."

After school, I spent most of the afternoon pacing around the house, trying to figure out exactly what to tell my mom about our mall trip.

I have the measles?

No, she'd send me straight to bed and then drag me to nasty Dr. Kaychuck, whose idea of fun is to pinch my cheeks and tell me how cute I am — just before jabbing me with the sharpest needle he's got.

Maybe I could take a cue from Zach:

"Mom, how can I buy new jeans when I know they're made by toddlers in sweatshops?"

Just one problem: I'd probably still end up at the mall with my mother, and we'd each come home with a new pair of burlap pants.

Anyway, you can see why I was so nervous. Part of me was hoping that nighttime would never arrive. Ben, on the other hand, couldn't wait for the afternoon to pass. Ever since he'd come home, he'd been pacing around the kitchen, checking his watch approximately every two and a half minutes.

What was he waiting for? Well, he was a sixteen-year-old boy who'd just gotten his learner's permit — what do you think he was waiting for?

The phone rang.

"Dad?" Ben said anxiously into the receiver, after picking it up midway through the first ring.

"Hey, Ben, I won't be able to give you a driving lesson today," Dad told him apologetically.

"Oh," Ben replied simply. But that one syllable contained a whole world of teen angst.

"I'm sorry, son," Dad told him briskly. "I've got an important meeting I can't miss."

Ben hung up the phone, sat down, and his shoulders slumped.

"Sure," he muttered bitterly. "What meeting is more important than your own son?"

Since I happened to be passing through the kitchen at the time, on round thirty of my pacing through the house, I figured I could give him some help on that one.

"He must have another son somewhere else that he likes better," I suggested as I swung through the living room.

Okay, so it wasn't particularly helpful. But it sure was funny.

How was *I* supposed to know that he'd actually believe me . . . ?

Dad didn't have another family hidden away somewhere, of course.

But he also didn't have a business meeting.

While Ben was sitting at home sulking, imagining all that precious driving time he was missing, Dad was sneaking through a seedy back alley, looking for the man he was due to meet.

Finally, just as Dad was about to give up, he spotted the man's shadowy profile in the passenger's seat of a dusty blue car. The mysterious figure beckoned to him. Nervous, but resolved, Dad approached the car and, taking a deep breath, pulled open the door. He slipped into the driver's seat, then turned to face the man he'd come to see.

"Hi," he said timidly, clearing his throat. "Are you . . . ?"

"Stick Shifty of Stick Shifty's Driving School?" the passenger finished for him with a cheerful grin. "You're looking at him."

Stick Shifty was . . . shifty-looking, with squinty eyes, week-old stubble, and a rumpled shirt.

"I've done this before," Dad boasted. "I just . . . need a little refresher. I'm gonna teach my son how to drive a stick shift."

Stick Shifty pretty much ignored him. His look said he'd seen it *all* before.

"Yeah, don't worry," he assured Dad. "Stick Shifty's never lost a student yet! Now, hold down the clutch, and start the car."

Dad bit his lower lip and stared down at the steering wheel, then held down the clutch and turned the ignition.

*SCREEEEEEEECH.*

The car let out a horrible squeal, a painful grinding screech, a few chugs and whimpers, and then finally, mercifully, fell silent.

Dad smiled sheepishly at Stick Shifty and took his hands off the wheel.

"That's probably a bad sound, huh?"

Stick Shifty glared at him and shook his head in disgust.

"You've never driven stick a day in your life, have you?" he asked with a groan.

"I do other things really well," Dad sputtered, talking fast and loud as if he had something to prove. Which I guess he did. "I can play the drums. You should see me bowl. And when I barbecue —"

"And I'm sure it's delicious." Stick Shifty cut him off, sounding a little patronizing and more than a little bored. "You know you're paying by the hour — right?"

"Addie, let's go!" Mom called. She was standing by the door, holding her purse. Okay, so I'd kind of left the whole truth-telling thing to the last minute. Can you blame me? "The mall closes at nine. If we get there soon enough, we can paint another set of mugs for Grandma!"

You know, I kind of think Grandma has enough mugs. We paint her one *every* time we go to the mall. And we've been doing it since I was seven!

"Yeah, Mom, about shopping . . ."

Before I could continue, our dog, Nancy, came trotting through the kitchen — stinking like she'd just taken a roll in the mud.

"Nancy! Whew!" Mom exclaimed, sniffing the air and grimacing. "You need a bath!"

Nancy ran out of the room for a minute, and when she came back in, she was dragging her little inflatable kiddie pool behind her. She ran off again, and returned with a hose. On the third trip, she brought back a loo-fah. Then she started giving herself a bath.

I know that everyone thinks their dog is the smart-est dog in the world . . . but you've got to admit, in my case, it might actually be true.

"What were you saying, honey?" Mom asked, when we'd both stopped admiring our shaggy, golden-haired dog.

"About shopping," I repeated. "I can't. I —"

This was it. The moment of truth.

Well, not really *truth* . . .

"I have this thing," I said vaguely, stalling for time.

"A thing?"

"Yeah, a thing." I nodded furiously. Maybe if I looked confident, and sounded confident, I would actually start feeling confident. Or at least stop feeling like a big, fat liar. "A study group. A group for studying," I babbled. This whole lying thing was harder than it looked. Or maybe I just needed more practice. "Big test tomorrow. Hugely massive."

"Oh. Well." Mom looked so disappointed. I knew it — I *knew* she'd be crushed. I looked away, not wanting to see her big blue eyes well up with tears. Not that she was crying, but I figured that might come next. After all, I was robbing her of the chance to bond with her only daughter. "We'll go shopping over the weekend," she said.

"Yeah, sure." I shrugged. I wasn't about to make another promise and get myself stuck in the same situation all over again.

"Don't work too hard," she urged me. Oh, no, now she was going to start being *nice* to me? Like I could feel any worse? "Lately, you've been spending so much time lying, you barely have any time to lie."

Uh, *what*! Did I hear that right? I blinked and gave myself a little shake. Mom was still talking, and all I could hear was . . .

"Lie, lie! Lie lie lie, lie. Lie lie lie. Lie lie, lie lie lie — lie lie . . . and after that, we can go for dim sum!"

My mother was grinning at me, and I realized that whatever I'd heard had sprung out of my own guilty imagination. So I smiled back, pretending that I had heard what she actually said in reality. Pretending that, inside, I wasn't feeling like the worst daughter on the face of the earth.

"Yeah, great," I mumbled. "Thanks, Mom."

Nancy padded back into the room, freshly washed and blow-dried, and decked out in a red, white, and blue bow.

"Aww, Nancy, you put on your Fourth of July bow!" Mom waved the dog away. "But it's autumn, so go find something in a brown leaf pattern." She smiled indulgently at me and shook her head. "That dog has no sense of style."

Under other circumstances, I might have stood up for Nancy. After all, she's my dog. And, besides, I thought the bow looked cute, no matter what month it was. But I couldn't say anything. I was afraid that if I opened my mouth again, the real reason I didn't want to go to the mall would pop out. So, instead, I just waved silently at my mom — and slipped out the door.

*     *     *

It took me about fifteen minutes to walk to *Juice!* — and I spent every one of those minutes kicking myself for lying to my mother.

*Liar! Liar! Liar!* a little voice in my head shouted with every step.

I hoped that when I finally made it to the café, seeing Geena and Zach would make me forget the whole liar thing. But after a half hour of sitting there silently, gulping down my smoothie, I had to admit it wasn't working.

"See, don't you feel better that you're not wasting your youth?" Geena asked, taking a delicate sip from her Berry Blast-off.

I barely heard her. I was still picturing my mother's face. Only in my imagination, it was streaked with tears.

"She was so disappointed," I moaned. "I wanted to die."

"That's the spirit!" Geena cheered.

Before I could point out that my big lie wasn't really cause to celebrate, some guy slammed into our table and knocked his drink all over it. Geena and I both squealed and hopped out of our seats to get away from the smoothie oozing across the table.

Geena did a quick outfit-check to make sure nothing had spattered onto her shirt. "Watch what you're doing, you big —" That's when she got a good look at the guy who had bumped into us.

He was tall and built, with adorable dimples and curly hair that you knew would be supersoft to the touch. Even I had to admit, he was supercute.

"I'm so sorry," the guy told us, arms spread in apology. "I didn't get any juice on you, did I?"

"Yeah, just a little —" I began, thinking that, cute or not, he didn't sound nearly sorry enough. But Geena elbowed me in the ribs before I could go any further. "Ow!"

"No, not a drop!" Geena chirped, batting her eyes at him. "We're totally clean. *Right*, Addie?" She shot me a death glare — one that I knew better than to disobey.

"Totally," I agreed, smiling through gritted teeth, and wincing at the pain in my ribs.

"Let me make it up to you," the guy said, flashing us a hundred-watt grin.

"Oh, really, you don't need to —" Geena stopped herself and looked thoughtful for a moment. "What did you have in mind?"

"Why don't you guys come and hang out with me

and some friends next week?" the clumsy cutie offered. "On Thursdays, we like to go to this place called the —"

"Point!" Geena and I cried together. I couldn't believe it. The Point? Suddenly, this night was looking a whole lot better.

"Yeah," Geena added, once we'd both recovered our cool. She was trying to sound like she didn't care one way or another. But it totally wasn't working. "I think we've heard of it."

"Oh, we've heard of it," Zach cut in, shaking his head in disgust. I have to admit, I'd almost forgotten he was there. "And we are *not* interested — *ow!*"

This time, Geena elbowed Zach in the stomach. *Good for her,* I thought.

"He's not interested," Geena said brusquely, stepping in front of Zach. "We are."

Our high school hero shrugged. "Okay, whatever. It's pretty mellow," he cautioned us. "Just a few people, listening to music."

"We love people!" I said eagerly. "And music. And being mellow."

I have to admit, I would have said anything — after all, this was *The Point.*

&starf;  &starf;  &starf;

There was only one thing that could have brought down my mood after that — the sight of my mother, standing in the doorway of *Juice!*, catching me red-handed. So the good news is, I didn't see her.

The bad news is, she saw me.

She was talking to Grandma on the phone as she walked in the door.

"Fine, Mom, I won't send you any more mugs," she conceded. "I'll sell them on eBay." There was a pause, and then she scrunched up her face in indignation. "Yes, I *do* think someone would pay money for them."

That's when she spotted me. She stopped short in her tracks and froze in the doorway. "Mom, I gotta go," she said into the phone, and snapped it shut before Grandma had a chance to respond.

Then she just stood there and watched me for a minute. Flirting with the high school guy, laughing with Geena, yelling at Zach. There was no studying in sight. The only way my lie could have been more obvious would have been if I were wearing a sign: ADDIE SINGER — BIG FAT LIAR.

Mom took a step toward our table — then stopped and thought better of it. She turned on her heel and walked out the door, slamming it behind her.

I looked up when I heard the noise — but by that time, she'd already disappeared.

When I got home, I was still walking on air, dreaming of going to The Point. The guy — turns out his name is Chad — had agreed to take us there on Thursday. I could barely wait. How was I ever going to stand the suspense?

"Hello, Addie," Mom greeted me when I came in. She was sitting on the sofa, reading a book and waiting for me.

"Hey, Mom," I said, trying to sound casual.

"How was your study group?" she asked, glaring at me.

Uh-oh.

"Oh, great!" I said in my perkiest voice, fumbling for something normal-sounding to say. "I'm sure I'll be getting a pretty hefty scholarship to college, so —"

"I saw you at *Juice!*" she interrupted, in a low, quiet voice.

"Oh." I didn't know what to say. I tried to think of another lie I could tell that would make things better. But this time around, I came up empty.

"Why didn't you just tell me the truth?" she asked, her eyes filled with disappointment.

"I didn't want to make you feel bad," I admitted.

"Well, that's too bad . . . because now I feel really bad about grounding you," she said.

"What?!" I yelped. Didn't I get *any* credit for owning up to what I'd done? And, really, what had I done? I'd just been trying to spare her feelings. Was that so bad?

"Addie, you lied to me," she pointed out.

"I didn't have a choice!" I cried. I was fighting for my life now. Well, at least my social life. "You're always pressuring me to do things with you," I blurted. "And we just don't have anything in common."

Maybe if I'd been looking at Mom, I would have seen how shocked and hurt she looked to hear that. And maybe I would have stopped myself before I went any further. But I was too angry and upset to be paying attention to her expression. So I kept going.

"Don't you have any friends your own age to hang out with?"

"Well, forgive me for wanting to hang out with my daughter!" Mom snapped, her face getting red with some anger of her own.

"Well, forgive *me* for wanting to do my own thing!" I shouted back.

"Go to your room!" Mom thundered.

"Gladly!" I shot back and stormed away. I ran up the stairs to my room and slammed the door behind me as hard as I could. A moment later, I heard my mom's door slam shut, too.

And then, the house was silent.

At least Mom didn't take away my TV privileges. I spent the next night bumming around on the couch, staring aimlessly at the screen. Ben was slumped down next to me, looking about as bad as I felt.

"It's all Mom's fault," I said dejectedly, flipping through the channels. "It's not like I wanted to fight."

Ben just ignored me. He had his own problems.

"I think Dad's avoiding me," he said, thinking aloud.

"She just doesn't get it," I complained. "I'm thirteen now. I'm gonna be doing things on my own."

"At this rate, I'll never learn how to drive," Ben whined. I barely heard him. "I'll be pushing my kids to Little League in a shopping cart."

We didn't know it, but upstairs in their room, Mom and Dad were having a little gripe session of their own.

"Ben's getting suspicious," Dad said, setting down his book, *Stick Shift for Dummies*. "He knows I'm avoiding him."

"Maybe I was too harsh with Addie," Mom said, setting down her own book.

"Why can't he just learn on my car?" Dad asked, running a hand through his hair in exasperation. "What's wrong with my car? It smells a little, but the engine's still good. . . ."

"Then again, she *did* lie," Mom reconsidered.

Downstairs, Ben and I were still lost in our own world of complaints.

"Sometimes I just don't *get* her," I sighed.

"Parents," Ben and I said at the same time.

"Sometimes I just don't *get* her," Mom said.

Dad shook his head and picked up his book again.

"Kids," they both said in unison.

I went to bed early that night. (There's not much else to do when you're grounded, after all.) But I couldn't sleep. After tossing and turning for an hour or so, I threw off my covers and got out of bed. It was no use. I just couldn't relax, not when my mind was running around in circles. At times like this, there was really only one thing that could calm me down.

I got my guitar out of the closet and plopped back down on my bed, already strumming some chords. The more I played, the better I felt. And the more certain I got. Like my song said:

*No more book club,*
*No more Nut Jim,*
*I'm not painting mugs again.*
*I'm thirteen, yeah!*
*Thirteen years old.*
*Don't need to do what I'm told . . .*

Don't need to do what I'm told. . . . Now, *that* was an interesting idea.

"Are you sure?" Geena whispered, leaning over toward my desk the next day at school. I checked on our teacher — she was still writing on the board, her back turned to us.

"I'm sure," I whispered back. Geena peered at me incredulously, and I could tell she didn't believe I would really go through with it. But she'd find out soon enough. "I don't want to waste my youth," I explained, resolve filling my quiet voice. "I want to go to The Point. But I'll need a major plan to get out of Mom's lockdown."

All I had come up with so far was a *Mission Impossible*–style breakout:

*Dressed in black from head to toe, I pressed myself against the wall. Were they on to me? I looked to the left. Then to the right. Nothing. The coast was clear. I pushed aside my bedroom curtains — only to find metal bars lining the windows. I was trapped! Like a rat in a cage. Like a prisoner in solitary. Like Geena in detention. I could feel the walls closing in on me. I tiptoed to the door and threw it open — more bars!*

*But I was crafty. I'd gotten out of stickier situations than this. I just had to rely on my wits — and my spoon. It was hidden inside an old book, buried beneath my mattress. The warden never suspected a thing. Clutching the spoon like it was my life preserver, I opened the closet door and shoved my clothes aside. There it was. My escape route. I'd been digging through the plaster, through the insulation, through the retaining wall, and now, with a little more chiseling . . .*

*"Yes!" I was through.*

*I climbed through the hole and tunneled my way through to the rendezvous point. Out of the house, across town, all the way to Juice! I got into position and — CRACK! I knocked a hole through the floorboard and leaped through, landing in the middle of* Juice!, *just in front of Geena and Chad's table.*

*I was out, and it was glorious. I let out a wild yell of triumph and exhilaration.*

*"I'm free, Mother!" I crowed, my cry echoing through the room. I held the spoon, my instrument of victory, aloft in celebration. "FREEEEEEEE!"*

*Chad and Geena, covered in plaster and dust from the hole in the ceiling, looked over at me in shock and awe.*

*"Hey, guys," I said, playing it cool — this was, after all, just another day's work for Addie Singer, Super Spy. "What up? Smoothies for the table?"*

Perhaps you can see why I needed to come up with a better plan.

"Do whatever you have to do," Geena advised. "But wear something cute. And not blue, 'cause that's what I'll be wearing."

So my real breakout didn't exactly follow my fantasy scenario — but it was still the most daring escape I'd ever made. Mom spent most of the afternoon in the living room, meditating. She sat in the middle of the floor, legs crossed, arms resting on the edge of her knees, her back perfectly straight. She had her *Soothing*

*Sounds of the Sea* CD on and was making whooshing noises along with the stereo.

"I'm home," I said as I passed through on my way upstairs.

"Want me to make you a snack?" she asked, in the soft, soothing voice she uses when she's trying to "center" herself. This was the first time we'd really talked since our big fight. I couldn't believe she was being so nice to me. Maybe it was all just a ploy to make me feel guilty. Maybe she knew I was up to something and she was hoping to guilt me into behaving. Well, nice try, Mom, but it wasn't going to work.

"No, thanks," I replied. "I'm going up to my room to do some homework and shouldn't be disturbed for the rest of the evening."

"Fine," she said. "If you're hungry, I made plenty of mushroom caps. Unless you think those are lame, too."

Ugh, there's that guilt again.

I plodded up the stairs, trying to forget the whole conversation. And Mom just went back to meditating.

It took me a while to pick out exactly the right outfit — I mean, what do you wear to the coolest place in the world? What kind of outfit really says, "I'm totally cool enough to be here," without saying, "I'm trying really hard because I'm afraid I'm not cool enough to be here?"

My cute jeans with the flower patch on the knee? Too sixth grade.

My yellow twinset and matching skirt? Too country club.

The pink sequined skirt Geena gave me for my birthday? Just . . . too much.

Finally, I settled on my favorite outfit — a light pink tank and a hot-pink skirt. I even had a little pink purse to match. Checking myself out in the mirror, I decided it was supercute. I was totally Point-worthy.

Okay, problem one: solved.

Now on to problem two: getting past the warden.

I tiptoed down the stairs — Mom was still meditating in the living room.

"Whooooooooosh," she chanted, her eyes closed.

I crept past her, my feet padding softly against the hardwood floor. Just a few feet now between me and freedom. One quiet step, then another, then another — and then I was there, the back door. All I had to do was open it. . . .

*SQUEEEEaK!*

I leaped away from the door and froze. Mom's

body tensed up, and she fell silent, listening. I stood a few steps behind her, perfectly still, praying that she wouldn't turn around. *Finally,* she shut her eyes again, and I could tell by her rhythmic breathing that she was back to her meditation. How was I going to get out of here? Geena and Chad were waiting for me at *Juice!* — but I knew they wouldn't wait forever. And no way was I traipsing back up to my room and letting Geena go to The Point without me.

That's when I spotted it.

My escape route. And it was perfect.

I knelt on the ground and began to crawl forward, slowly, silently. Then I poked my head through the little flap at the bottom — Nancy's dog door. I took one last look back at Mom ... and then, with a deep breath, I made a break for it.

I squeezed myself through the tiny space, wriggling forward, inch by inch, and then, suddenly, I stopped short. Half of me was outside, half of me was inside — and all of me was stuck. But I'd come this far. I only needed to go a couple of feet farther.

I held my breath and pushed myself forward with all my might.

*RIIIIIIP!*

I'd made it through all right — but my skirt was

still on the other side of the doggy door. And I was kneeling outside on the porch wearing nothing but my pink shirt and my days-of-the-week underwear.

On the other hand, I was out of the house. (It always helps to look on the bright side, right?) I reached my hand back through the doggy door and felt around for my skirt.

When I finally made it to *Juice!*, Chad and Geena were waiting for me impatiently, as I'd expected. I was just glad they hadn't left without me.

"What took you so long?" Geena asked. She kept her voice light, but I knew she was totally relieved to see me. I bet she was pretty surprised, too — I'd never done anything like sneaking out of the house before. (Usually, I barely have the nerve to sneak downstairs to the cookie jar.)

"Let's get out of here," Chad said, standing up from his table and striding toward the door before I could answer.

Geena started to follow him out, but I pulled her aside.

"I can't go like this," I hissed, gesturing down at myself. My skirt had ripped on its way through the doggy door and was practically in two pieces. I had a tight grip on the waistband — but if I let go for a second, all of *Juice!* would see that I was wearing my Tᴜᴇsᴅᴀʏ underwear on a Thursday. This was so *not* the way I wanted to make my first appearance at The Point.

"Addie, Chad has a car," Geena said slowly. "He's taking us to the fountain of all maturity. You are *so* going."

"I ripped my skirt," I pointed out to her, taking my hand away from the giant tear for a minute so she could inspect the damage.

"Don't worry," Geena assured me. "I've brought paper clips."

Did she say paper clips?

Geena grabbed my hand and pulled me out of the café. We were off. Off to Chad's car, to The Point, to the fountain of all maturity. And I was more than ready, except . . .

Seriously, did she really say paper clips?

While I was speeding toward The Point, wondering if anything else was going to go wrong, Ben was hatching a secret plan of his own. He lay in wait all afternoon, crouched on the couch under a blanket, just waiting for his prey. After about an hour, Dad walked through the door. Ben steeled himself and, as soon as Dad set foot in the living room, Ben jumped off the couch and threw the blanket over Dad's head.

"Aha!" he cried, grabbing Dad in a bear hug to keep the blanket on tight. "Busted."

Ben's trap had worked — but, unfortunately, it wasn't much of a trap. Dad shrugged him away easily and pulled off the blanket.

"Ben?" he asked, looking at his son as if he'd lost his mind. "Why did you throw a blanket on my head?"

"Don't change the subject," Ben insisted, circling Dad to keep him off balance. "I figured it all out. The sneaking around, the avoiding me. You have another family, don't you?"

Okay, so maybe I should take a little of the blame for Ben's delusions. But, like I said, I was just teasing him — who knew he'd take me seriously.

"What?!" Dad asked incredulously.

"That's why you haven't had time to teach me how to drive," Ben accused him. "Admit it."

Dad just stared at him for a minute. Ben glared back, refusing to let him talk his way out of this one. As far as Ben was concerned, I guess, Dad had been caught red-handed.

Finally, Dad pulled something out of his pocket and dangled it in front of Ben: a set of keys.

"Your mother finally left me her keys today," Dad informed him, shaking his head. "I was just going upstairs to look for you."

"Oh." Ben looked a little embarrassed — for about ten seconds. Then he grinned. "Cool." He snatched the keys out of Dad's hand and headed for the door.

Dad watched him go, probably wondering whether he really wanted to sit in a car with Ben behind the wheel. But then he sighed and followed Ben out the door, resigned to his fate.

"Cool."

Back to the important stuff, i.e., *my* life. If you're anything like me, you're probably dying of curiosity to hear about The Point. So I won't keep you in suspense anymore. The Point was — well, how can I put this?

Totally lame.

Lamesville.

Lamer than a field trip to Nut Jim with the mother-daughter book club.

Here's all I knew about The Point ahead of time: It was a secret, isolated spot filled with cool people doing cool things.

Here's what I figured out about The Point five seconds after we got there: Everything I thought I knew was wrong.

The Point was isolated, all right, but only because there was no reason for anyone in town to set foot there. It was just an old abandoned park, surrounded by a rickety barbed-wire fence and filled with rusted playground equipment. There were plenty of older kids there, high school kids — but it wasn't long before I learned my second lesson about the world. Being older doesn't automatically make you cooler. (You'd think with Ben as my big brother, I would have figured that out a lot sooner.)

Don't believe me? Check out Exhibit A, a smug jock who had "cool dude" written all over him. In his own handwriting.

"What's up, man?" the football dude asked Chad, giving him one of those half back-slap things that guys do when they don't actually want to hug.

"Not much," Chad said, trying to sound bored, like he was waiting for something more interesting to happen. "You?"

"Chillin'," the dude replied. "Watch me make this soda come out through my nose!"

He chugged his soda, and then, sure enough, put a finger over one nostril and squirted a steady stream of soda out the other.

"Oh, dude, that's gross!" Chad exclaimed, eyes wide in admiration. "You rule!"

Well, Geena had been right — thanks to Chad, we'd found the fountain of all maturity. The *nose* fountain of all maturity. And if he got a little more squirting range on the next chug, we'd be getting a maturity shower.

I turned to Geena, expecting to see the same disgusted look on her face, but I guess she wasn't ready to give up the dream.

"So, Chad," she said charmingly, smiling up at him. "Are you named for —"

"Yo, Venus!" Chad called, running over toward this beautiful blond high school girl. Chad swept her into a hug, then slung an arm around her and walked off toward the other side of the park. Well, that was great. Just great.

"Zach was right," I complained, dejected.

"About jeans and sweatshops?" Geena asked in confusion. "No, he wasn't. He got a rash from those burlap pants."

How could she have clothes on the brain at a time like this?

"About this *place*," I corrected her. "It is totally —"

I fell silent suddenly, as my skirt started to fall down, revealing my days-of-the-week underwear. So much for paper clips.

"What up, Tuesday!" the jock shouted at me. Total humiliation.

"Lame." I pulled my skirt back up and a hot, red blush was blooming across my face. "The Point is lame."

Don't get me wrong. I know all about humiliating myself in front of . . . well, everyone. That's what happens when you're a total klutz. But losing my skirt in front of everyone at The Point was definitely a new low.

"Don't worry," Geena said. "By next week, TUESDAY underwear will be all the rage."

Somehow, I doubted it. But my protests were drowned out by the sound of tires squealing out of the parking lot.

"Okay," Geena said, squinting into the distance to make out the car. "Our ride just left."

Left? Our ride *left*? The Point had suddenly turned into The Point of No Return. I started hyperventilating at the thought of having to stick around for more "fun."

"What are we going to do, Geena?" I asked in horror.

"You got any ideas?" Geena asked.

Better than hopping into a car with our favorite nose-squirting football player? I could think of a few. I would *live* at The Point before I drove anywhere with some random weirdo — and I'd make sure Geena lived there with me.

But maybe it wouldn't have to come to that, I realized. There was one other option, and while it wasn't a great one, it was kind of all we had.

I took out my cell phone and dialed the number, waiting for the familiar voice to pick up the phone. This wasn't going to be pretty. But at this point, it didn't seem like things could get much worse.

The phone rang twice, and then she picked up. I took a deep breath.

"Mom?"

Mom was home alone because Ben and Dad had finally set out on their very first driving lesson. Ben had driven about three blocks, and so far, so good.

"Okay, son," Dad said, trying to sound calm and confident. It wasn't too convincing. "Come on, just ease up on the clutch while concurrently pressing down on the gas pedal." He waited. The car didn't move. "Go ahead," he urged Ben gently.

A loud honk sounded from behind them.

"Get movin'!" the guy stuck behind them shouted, not so gently.

Ben clutched the steering wheel, his knuckles turning white.

"Now, son, you can do it," Dad assured him. "Easy, easy. Gently let up on the clutch —"

"I can't do it!" Ben suddenly blurted, pushing himself away from the wheel.

"Move it!" came another angry voice from behind them.

"Please, Dad," Ben begged, "just take over."

Dad stared at him in horror and didn't move.

The angry honkers were getting restless.

"Uh . . . okay," Dad muttered, unfastening his seat belt. "I'll . . . take over."

They got out of the car and switched places as quickly as they could, and then — nothing. Dad just sat there for a moment, hands on the wheel, staring straight ahead.

"What's the holdup here?!" someone else shouted from behind him.

Dad must have realized that sitting still could be just as dangerous as driving — at least when you have a horde of angry drivers stuck behind you. So he shifted the car into gear. The car didn't move — but the gears did, with a loud crunching and squealing.

"Uh, Dad? You're grinding the gears," Ben pointed out.

"I can hear the gears!" Dad snapped, trying again. More crunching, more squealing, more grinding — no moving. Then, suddenly, the car sputtered and lurched forward. And then it died.

"Dad, what's wrong?" Ben asked in alarm.

Dad threw up his arms in frustration, giving up.

"Ben, I can't drive a stick shift," he finally admitted, talking over the honking and shouting that was filling the air. "I never could. That's why I've been putting this whole thing off. I didn't tell you because I didn't want to let you down."

Dad waited for the explosion, but Ben just looked down at his lap.

"Well . . . I have something to tell you, too," he said softly.

"You're the one who stunk up my car?" Dad asked. For some reason, he sounded surprised.

"Well, yeah," Ben said, shrugging as if that were too obvious to discuss. "But that's not it." He hesitated, still looking away. "I didn't really pass my driver's test. I flunked it."

"It's okay, son," Dad said in an understanding tone, clapping Ben on the shoulder. "You can always take the test again —"

"Not this year," Ben corrected him. "I've already taken it ten times. That's the max."

"Ten times?" Dad asked in shock. (Though, again, I don't really know why he was so surprised. This is Ben we're talking about here.) He chuckled in spite of himself. "Are you sure you were taking the test in English?"

"Dad!"

"I mean . . ." Hearing Ben's pathetic tone, Dad snapped back into Reassuring Dad Mode. "You'll take the test again and you'll pass it, eventually. And you're gonna be a good driver. I can tell."

A gray sedan maneuvered around them, honking all the way.

"Get that can moving before I kick your butt!" the driver shouted as she passed by, sticking her head out the window and shaking her fist at our car.

"Oh, hi, Karen!" Dad called back cheerfully, recognizing her from the mother-daughter book club. He gave her a friendly wave.

He didn't get one in return.

"It's KAHR-ren!"


Mom and I didn't speak for the entire ride home. Silence hung in the air between us, so heavy I felt like it was crushing me. Geena, sitting in the backseat, noticed the tension, so she did what she always does when she's nervous: talked. And talked, and talked. She chattered the whole way home, trying to warm the icy air with the sound of her voice. It didn't work.

". . . and then he said he thought I might need

braces," she was saying as the three of us walked into the house. "But, hello, I already have a retainer, so I say, let's give it some time, right?"

Mom gave me a look, and I gave Geena a look, and Geena looked over our shoulders, out the window. She was probably wishing she was somewhere — anywhere — else.

"Okay, well, that was fun," she chattered, forcing a smile and backing away. "I can just walk home from here." She mimed making a phone call in my direction and whispered, "Call me." Then she scurried out the back door. And Mom and I were left alone. I wondered which of us was supposed to start. Mom said nothing, just raised an eyebrow and waited. I guess that meant it was my turn.

"Before you say anything, I'm sorry for lying and for sneaking out," I began, realizing for the first time how incredibly guilty I felt. Not just for the lying, but for everything. "Really, really sorry. And I'm totally self-grounding. Three weeks minimum."

Gradually, a smile warmed the cold look in Mom's eyes.

"One week will do," she conceded. "And we're going to have a serious talk about you sneaking out." I nodded, looking down at my feet. I couldn't complain — it seemed like I was getting off easy. "But you did the right thing in calling me," she continued.

"I'm sorry about hating book club and every-thing," I told her, hoping she would understand I meant *everything*, including all those horrible things I'd said to her.

Maybe she did, because her smile got a little big-ger, and she gave me a gentle shrug.

"Well, you're growing up," she reminded me. "It's normal for you to want to do things on your own. We'll figure it out. We've just got to be *honest* with each other about stuff like that."

I raised my head to meet her eyes and solemnly nodded. I wanted her to know that I was serious. This whole double-life thing was over, starting now. I was going to be the real Addie, all the time. And that meant telling the truth.

"So . . . that was the infamous Point?" Mom asked with a mischievous grin. She knew all about how desper-ate I'd been to get invited there.

I just laughed and rolled my eyes.

"Looked like a dump to me," Mom commented, wrinkling her nose.

"Totally lame," I agreed.

And then she gave me a big hug, and I guess we were officially made up. We spent the rest of the afternoon baking cookies. I never would have thought that playing board games with my mom could be a cooler way to spend an afternoon than going to The Point. But, hey, I've been wrong before!

Let's just hope that I'll never be so wrong again.

Back in the car, Dad and Ben were having their own family-bonding moment.

"I'm really glad we got all this out in the open," Dad said, still in the driver's seat as the car sped toward home.

"Yeah, me, too," Ben agreed, nodding in relief. "Hey, you wanna go for smoothies?"

"Oh, I'd love to!" Dad replied. He took his hands off the steering wheel and rubbed them together in anticipation. And why not? After all, there was no reason for them to be on the wheel — you couldn't do much steering when your car was perched on the flatbed of a tow truck.

Come on, how else were they supposed to get the car out of the road and back to our driveway? It's not like either of them could *drive*!

"Yeah, just as soon as we get home and get my

car, I'm with you," Dad added, already imagining the sweet refreshing taste of a Very Merry Berry smoothie. "Maybe we can get this guy to stop at *Juice!* Hey, can you stop?" he called out the window, toward the cab of the tow truck. "Helloooooooo!?"

And that's how I ended up grounded for the second time in a month. I can't say that it was worth it to see The Point — though at least now I don't have to waste any more brain space wondering how to score myself an invite. And at least Mom and I finally got everything out in the open. It feels really good to be honest with her again. Plus, I got all the inspiration I needed to write a new song:

> *Growin' up is like drivin' a stick shift,*
> *Everything concurrently and that's the trick.*
> *If you do it all wrong, then you might just stall,*
> *You'll be whippin' out your phone*
>           *and givin' Mom a call.*
> *Oh, you're never too old to give Mom a call.*
> *You're not a fool, you're still cool. . . .*

Mom came into my room as I was still playing, fooling around with the lyrics.

"Nice song," she commented, setting down a basket of clean laundry on my bed. "Fixed your skirt."

I sat up on the bed and she handed it to me — all in one piece.

"It looks perfect!" I cried. Sometimes, my mom is amazing.

"Well, after fifteen years of making Halloween costumes . . ." She started absentmindedly folding the rest of the laundry as she spoke. "You know what I was thinking this year? That I could make you this cowgirl outfit kind of thing, 'cause, uh . . ."

Her voice trailed off as she saw my expression. It's not like I made a face or anything, at least not on purpose, it's just . . . a cowgirl costume? It was so babyish. So *not* what I was going for this year.

"Are you, uh, going trick-or-treating this year?" Mom asked, keeping her voice neutral.

"Of course," I reassured her. Halloween is always my favorite holiday. Costumes, staying up past my bedtime, and all the candy I can eat? I'd be crazy to pass that up. "I was thinking more of a supermodel vampire-slayer kind of thing," I explained. "That way, I could use my own clothes."

Mom looked down at the clothes she was folding and nodded. She was trying to look like she didn't really care one way or another, but I knew she did. After all, she'd been helping me with my Halloween costume every year since I was born — it was just one of those things we always did together. Like a tradition, you know? And who was I to mess with tradition?

"But, um . . ." I began hesitantly.

"What?"

"You could make me a cape," I suggested.

It was totally the right thing to say. Mom brightened up instantly.

"Oh, sure," she chirped, sitting down beside me on the bed. "You know, we could go shopping tomorrow after school and buy a bolt of sateen."

"But — tomorrow's book club," I reminded her. See, the old Addie would have just let her forget. But not me, not now. I'd promised to be honest, and that's just what I was going to do. Even if it meant another endless hour of book club. And I do mean endless.

"Uh." Mom raised her eyebrows. "I'm kinda over book club. *Kahr*-ren and *Breen*-da are *really* annoying."

I rolled my eyes. Tell me about it.

"You could slay *them* first," Mom suggested with a tiny smirk. As we laughed together, I remembered how much fun we always had hanging out. And I was a little glad this whole growing-up thing didn't automatically mean *that* had to change.

That night, I added another verse to my song:

*Mom promised to never take me back to Nut Jim,*
*As long as I don't sneak out*
  *of the doggy door again.*
*One thing I know, once and for all,*
*You're never too old to give your mom a call.*
*You're not a fool, you're still cool!*

I guess I just realized that Mom and I still have some things in common after all. I mean, even though we sometimes argue, I know I'm lucky, 'cause she's pretty cool.

You know — for a mom.

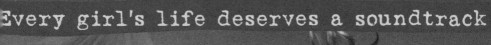